THE OVERALL BOYS IN SWITZERLAND

Eulalie Osgood Grover

THREE CHEERS FOR EUROPE

It was the first day of summer, and it was the last day of the ocean trip.

Jack and Joe, two Overall Boys, had crossed the big Atlantic. They were now sailing into a strange city, in a strange country, with a strange language.

The city was Antwerp. The country was Belgium, and the language was—well, almost anything one cared to speak, French or German or Dutch or English.

Jack said he should try English first. Then, if people did not understand him, he should use the Dutch words which the Sunbonnet Babies had taught him. But if people did not understand him then, he should have to keep still, or talk with his hands.

"Oh! I shall not keep still," said Joe. "I shall speak everything all at once, French and German and Dutch and English. You just watch me!"

"Ho! ho!" laughed Jack. "We will watch you, and so will all the people in Antwerp. But now watch that great houseboat. I believe it is like the boat Molly and May's Uncle Dirk owns. A family is living on it. They have a canary bird and a dog and a cat and flowers, just as they have on Uncle Dirk's boat."

"I should rather go to Holland than to Switzerland," said Joe. "Let's ask the people on that houseboat to take us up to their Water Land."

"No, sir! I want to go to Switzerland," said Jack. "I want to see the great mountains all covered with snowbanks and forests and flowers. There is not a mountain in the whole of Holland."

"Look!" shouted Joe. "I see the first castle! We are sailing right up beside it. I wonder if a really, truly King and Queen are living in it."

"Of course," said Jack, "unless they have been killed and their castle turned into a prison or a museum."

"Do you suppose it has a dark dungeon under it?" asked Joe. "How I should like to see a real dungeon!"

"Come on, father is calling us," said Jack. "Our boat has stopped. It is time to get off."

"Oh! Perhaps father will take us into that old castle, Jack. Then we can see if it really has a dungeon under it," cried Joe.

So the Overall Boys said good-by to their friends on the ocean steamer. They said good-by to the Captain. They said good-by to the Cook. The Cook and the Captain were their special friends and they were specially sorry to leave them.

But the boys had something very important in their minds.

When the heavy plank was pulled over from the dock to the steamer, the two Overall Boys were the first to step on it. They ran as fast as they could run down the steep plank.

Everybody wondered why those two boys were running so hard. There was plenty of time. No one needed to run. But in a second everybody knew, for Joe was throwing his cap high into the air and shouting, "Hurrah for Europe! Three cheers for Antwerp!" And in half a second more Jack was throwing his cap high into the air and shouting three cheers for Europe, too.

Yes, the Overall Boys were the first in their party to step foot on Europe, and they were the first to give it three cheers.
Chauffer and cook

ON THE RIVER RHINE

The next few days were exciting ones for the Overall Boys.

Joe said he knew that he was dreaming, and his dreams were all about castles and kings and queens and strange languages.

Jack had to tell him very often that he was sailing up the beautiful river Rhine toward Switzerland, that the castles and the kings and the queens and the strange languages were really true.

"I know that the castles are really here," said Joe, "for I am counting them. Look at that great fort on the hill!"

"Yes," said Jack, "the Captain says if we were their enemies, the soldiers in that fort would not let our boat pass up the river."

"Well, I am glad we are not their enemies," said Joe. "I don't like the looks of the big guns peeping through those holes in the fort walls. I like the old castles better."

And so the Overall Boys sailed by castles and still more castles, which were built high on the banks above the river. Most of them were very old, so old they were falling to pieces.

Lower down on the river banks there were large vineyards, where the finest grapes were growing.

Their father told the boys strange stories about the people who once lived in these old castles. He told them about a beautiful sea maiden who used to sit on a high rock above the river combing her long, golden hair and singing sweet songs. He told how brave young men sailed their boats into the dangerous waters to listen to her songs, and were drowned.

Fortunately the maiden did not sing while the Overall Boys were passing her rock, so they went safely on their journey.

A little later Jack cried, "Come, Joe, the Captain is going to tell us a story."

"Is he going to tell it in some dreadful, strange language?" asked Joe.

"No, sir!" said Jack. "This Captain knows how to speak English."

"Hello!" called the Captain. "Do you boys like mice? Both of you do! Well, that is brave. I am going to tell you about a man who did not like mice.

"Do you see that large, round tower just ahead of us? It is built on a rock in the middle of the river. It is called the Mouse Tower. This is the reason why.

"Once upon a time—I cannot tell you just how long ago, but once upon a time—there lived a rich Bishop. He lived in a great castle up there on the river bank. He had fine farms, and he made much money. He filled many barns with his grain, and he kept his gold in strong boxes.

"A great many poor people lived near the rich Bishop. He should have taught them how to work and how to pray, but he did not. He did not even give them grain when they needed it, or gold that they might buy bread.

"One year when the people were very hungry, they begged the Bishop so hard for bread that he could not sleep. He said they were like a pack of hungry mice.

"At last the Bishop told the beggars to go to an empty barn near by, and he would soon satisfy their wants. So the people hurried into the barn, and waited for the Bishop to come. He came, but he did not bring them food or gold.

"Oh, no! The selfish Bishop told his servants to set fire to the old barn, and the poor people who were inside soon stopped crying for food.

"That night while the Bishop was asleep in his castle, he dreamed a strange dream. He dreamed that some hungry mice were eating a fine picture of himself which hung on his bedroom wall. He watched them until they had torn it all to pieces.

"Just then a servant ran into his room and wakened him.

"'O Bishop Hatto! Bishop Hatto!' cried the servant. 'The mice are coming. They are coming out of the hot ashes of the old barn which we burned last night. They have followed me up to your castle. You must run for your life.'

"So the Bishop jumped on his horse and rode down the hill as fast as he could ride, and the mice ran after him. When he came to the river the mice were almost upon him.

"The Bishop left his horse and jumped into a small boat. He rowed very hard until he came to that stone tower in the middle of the river.

"'Now,' said he, 'I am safely away from those miserable mice.'

"But he was not safely away from them, for the mice could swim.

"The Bishop shut himself into the tower and closed the doors and windows. But the mice could gnaw. They ran up the stone walls and gnawed through the wooden doors. Then they ran down the doors on the inside and found the wicked Bishop.

"How the Bishop wished that he had been kind to the poor, starving people. How he wished that he had given them food and gold when they needed it so much. Now it was too late. The hungry people had sent their spirits back in these hungry mice to punish him as he had punished them.

"And so the old stone tower has been called the Mouse Tower, or Bishop Hatto's Tower, ever since. Now, what do you think of that for a story?" asked the Captain.

"I tell you, I hope I never shall be such a mean old Bishop as he was!" said Joe.

"And I am glad he is not living now!" said Jack.

Soon the Overall Boys had sailed as far up the beautiful river Rhine as their big boat would take them. They had seen so many old castles, and they had heard so many strange stories about them, the boys felt as if they had just passed through a really, truly Fairyland—and perhaps they had.
castle on a hill

THE BEAR CITY

"Hello, Jack! Hello, Joe!" called the boys' father very early one morning. "Wake up! Wake up and give the bears their breakfast."

"Oh, dear! Where are we?" cried Joe. "I'm so sleepy! Where are the bears? I don't see any."

"I know where we are," said Jack. "We are in the city of Bern, where the bear cave is."

"Good! We are in Switzerland at last," cried Joe, running to the window. "But where is the snow? I thought the mountains in Switzerland were all covered with snow! These mountains are covered with green trees."

"These are not the real mountains, Joe," said Jack. "The great snow-covered mountains are farther away. I guess we shall see them before long. I heard some one say that, on a clear day, the view of the snow-covered Alps from this city is one of the finest in all Switzerland, and that the sunsets here are wonderful. But let's have our breakfast now."

"All right," said Joe. "Then let's be off to hunt for the bears. But why do the people keep bears right in the middle of their city?"

"Father says it is because a bear was killed on this spot just before the city was built," said Jack. "So the people named the city Bern. They have kept a few bears in a large pit here ever since, and that is more than four hundred years."

"Do let's hurry and find their cave!" cried Joe.

So the Overall Boys were soon hurrying through the busy streets of the Bear City. In the middle of many of the streets they saw fine, large fountains. Above the center of some of the fountains were the figures of famous men, while plants and flowers were growing in others.

In a few of the beautiful fountains women were doing their washing. They placed the soiled clothes on boards by the edge of the clear water. Then they soaped the clothes well, and pounded them with flat stones, and rinsed them up and down until they were quite clean.

It was certainly an odd way to do a family washing; at least, so the Overall Boys thought.

There was one fountain which interested the boys more than any of the others. Above the center of this fountain stood the stone figure of a strange looking man, who was holding a stone baby in his hands. He was about to bite the baby's head right off. Other babies were hanging from the ugly man's belt and peeping from his pockets.

It is called the fountain of the Child-eater, and naughty children never like to pass very near it. But the Overall Boys knew that the stone Child-eater could not hurt them, so they laughed at the old fellow and hurried on.

It was not long before the boys were racing across a great stone bridge leading to the deep hole in the ground where the bears lived. Joe reached the pit first.

"Hurrah! I see three of them," he cried, leaning over the high rail above the pit. "See that baby bear beg for something to eat! Go to the fruit stand, Jack, and buy some carrots to feed him. Father says bears like carrots."

The boys threw the carrots, one at a time, over the wall into the pit

So Jack ran to the fruit stand near by and bought a big bunch of carrots. The boys threw the carrots, one at a time, over the wall into the pit, and how they shouted and laughed to see the bears catch and eat them, just like big, brown boys.

Sometimes one bear would catch more than his share of the carrots. Then the other bears would chase him about until they made him climb up a tall tree in the middle of the pit. He did not dare to come down until his bear friends had eaten all they wanted. If he tried to do so, they chased him quickly back again.

"Look!" cried Joe. "I have found an orange in my pocket. I am going to throw it down to the bear that is waving his paw at me. Watch him catch it."

"Watch him!" shouted Jack. "He didn't catch it. The bear near him knocked him over as quick as a wink, and caught the orange himself."

"See, he is climbing up the tree with it! Isn't he a selfish old bear!"

"Look at the bear in the little pond of water," cried Jack. "He is playing ball with the other bear. Now the other bear has jumped into the pond, too. See them box each other's ears! And see them roll over and over in the water! Oh, I never, never saw anything so funny!"

"I believe they are real boys dressed up in bear skins," said Joe. "I never thought bears could act so much like boys."

"Mother says she never thought boys could act so much like bears," said Jack.

The boys watched the bears nearly all the forenoon. Joe said he hadn't laughed so much since his last football game in America. He wished that he could live in Bern always, and feed the bears every morning.

"I'm getting hungry myself," said Jack at last. "Let's buy some gingerbread bears to eat. There is a window full of them over in that store."

Then away the boys ran and bought gingerbread bears of all sizes—father bears and mother bears and little baby bears and dancing bears and stiff soldier bears.

Jack and Joe were sure they had never eaten anything in all their lives so good as those gingerbread bears.

"Come on, now!" cried Jack. "Father has some more fun for us. He wants us to go down the street with him to see a queer old clock tower."

"I know what it is," said Joe. "He told us about it the other day. We can hear the cock crow and see the bears parade, if we are there on time."

"Then let's run!" said Jack. So the boys raced around corners and under arches

"Then let's run!" said Jack. "It is almost twelve o'clock now."

So the boys raced back over the great stone bridge. They raced around corners and under arches and along covered sidewalks, until they came to a low tower which arched right over the sidewalk.
town clock just before noon
The boys reached the tower just as the large clock near the top said five minutes before twelve

The large round clock near the top of the tower said five minutes before twelve. On the wall below the clock sat a queer little bronze man holding an hourglass in his hand.

At the left of the man stood a bronze cock and at his right a bronze dragon. Suddenly the Overall Boys saw the cock flap his wings and wag his head and cry, "Cock-a-doodle-doo!"

A moment later two bronze giants up in the top of the tower struck the great bell with their hammers twelve times. The cock wagged his head and flapped his wings and again crowed, "Cock-a-doodle-doo!" Then a small clown rang a tiny bell and a procession of bears began marching just below the old man.

Some of the bears carried little guns and swords, and one bear rode on a tiny horse.

When the clock in the top of the tower stopped striking, the procession stopped marching, and the old man turned his hourglass upside down. The dragon wagged his head, and the cock crowed, "Cock-a-doodle-doo!" Then all was still. Yes, it was very still. The Overall Boys were thinking.

At last Joe said, "I wish I could take that clock back to America. I should like to show it to the Sunbonnet Babies. I am sure they didn't see anything half as strange as that in Holland."

"Well, they will have to come to Bern if they want to see it," said Jack. "You can't pack that great tower in your trunk."

"Father is calling us," said Joe. "He says we shall have just time to eat dinner before we must take the train. Where do you suppose we are going next?"

ABOVE THE CLOUDS

"See it pour! And just hear the thunder!" said Joe, looking out of the car window. "It sounds as if giants were rolling rocks down the mountain sides. I hope they will not hit our train."

"Look! The train is stopping," said Jack. "The conductor says we must all get out here and take another train. How can we change while it is pouring so hard!"

The rain was really pouring down so fast that umbrellas were of no use at all. But the Overall Boys ran to the end of the platform and climbed into the high front seat of a queer little car.

It was certainly the strangest car the boys had ever seen. It was built so that one end was much higher than the other end, and people had to go up some steps to get into it.

In a few moments the little train was moving slowly up the steep track.

"Where do you suppose we are going?" cried Joe. "I believe we are climbing right up the side of a mountain. My! How it rains! I guess we are up among the clouds."

"We shall soon be up above the clouds," said Jack. "We are climbing Mount Rigi. We are going to stay all night on the mountain, too."

And so it happened. The train was soon pulled up the steep mountain side until it was above the rain and the wet clouds. The sun was shining brightly up there, but the valleys below were covered with a thick white blanket.

At last the sun and the wind began to carry great pieces of the cloud blanket high into the sky. Through the openings in the clouds, below them the boys could see tiny villages and blue lakes.

And away down below, hanging in the soft white clouds, was a rainbow—all red and orange and yellow and green and blue and violet.

"Look! We are above the rainbow bridge!" cried Joe. "If only I could jump over on it, I could slide right down to the earth again."

"Why, you are on the earth now," said Jack.

"Oh, so I am! But isn't it wonderful up here!"

The boys watched the fluffy clouds blow far away, carrying the lovely rainbow with them. And they watched the great red sun drop down behind the snow-covered mountains in the west.
boys standing on lookout

The boys watched the fluffy clouds blow far away

Suddenly Joe cried, "Those mountains are on fire, Jack! Look! How can they burn when they are all covered with snow?"

"It looks as if the red-hot sun had set the world on fire this time, doesn't it?" cried Jack.

But it hadn't, though the mountains were rosy for a long time after darkness had come in the deep valleys below. The great round moon climbed slowly up the sky, and millions of stars peeped down at the boys.

They had never been so near the stars before. They were almost six thousand feet nearer than they were on the ocean steamer, and six thousand feet are more than a mile.

At last the boys were so tired they went into a small hotel, high on the mountain, and were soon tucked away in two narrow white beds. For a few moments they lay very still, then Joe whispered, "Jack, do you hear those bells tinkling, out on the mountain side?"

And Jack whispered, "Yes, Joe. They are cow bells. You know five thousand cows are pastured on this mountain in the summer time."

"From the sound, I guess they all wear bells, too," said Joe. "Isn't it lovely! The bells make me so sleepy."
fast asleep in bed

ON MOUNT RIGI

So the boys were lulled to sleep by the soft music of the tinkling cow bells. But very early next morning they were wakened by another kind of music. It was the clear call of an alpine horn at four o'clock in the morning.

The horn seemed to say, "Wake up! Wake up and see the beautiful sunrise!"

Although Jack was still half asleep, he shouted back, "All right! We'll be up in a jiffy." And they were.

Everybody hurried out to the mountain top to watch the great sun sail slowly up the sky.

"Look!" cried Joe. "Last night the sun went down behind those mountains over there, but now it is coming up away over here. How did it ever get around here?"

"Oh, you know, Joe!" said Jack. "The sun always sets in the west and rises in the east."

"But how can it go down on one side of the world and come up on the other?" asked Joe.

"Because the earth whirls around every twenty-four hours," said Jack. "In the morning our side of the earth is whirling toward the sun, and in the afternoon we are whirling away from it."

"Oh, dear! Are we whirling now?" cried Joe. "I thought the world was standing still. I thought it was the sun that was going around."

"The sun is going around, Joe, but so are we. Father says that our world is whirling faster right now than the fastest automobile can race," said Jack.

"My!" said Joe. "Is that what makes the wind blow so hard up here? Hold on, or we shall be blown off!"

"Just look at those cows!" shouted Jack. "They are being milked. Let's go and watch."

Then away the boys raced to a group of big, brown cows that were being milked not far away. Great pails full of the rich, creamy milk were carried into a little house near by.
boys having breakfast
She filled two tall mugs with warm milk and piled a plate with gingerbread cakes, and set before them

"How good it looks!" said Joe. "Let's ask if they will sell us a drink."

But they did not have to ask, for the old woman who lived in the tiny house saw the boys coming. She knew that they had not had any breakfast, so she filled two tall mugs with warm milk, then she piled a plate with gingerbread cakes, and set before them.

The boys were so hungry they ate two plates full of the gingerbread cakes, and they each drank two tall mugs of the warm milk. They thanked the old woman very kindly, and told her she had given them the best breakfast they had ever eaten.

By this time the sun was quite high in the sky. Large umbrellas were raised over small booths on the mountain top, where men and women were selling picture post cards and all sorts of queer little things—horns and whistles and small carved wooden men and bears.

The boys bought a number of things to take back to America with them, and they bought a dozen or more post cards to send to their friends. The very prettiest of these cards were sent to their own little brothers, Tim and Ted, and to the Sunbonnet Babies.

The boys each bought, also, a fine alpine stock to help them on their long tramps over the mountains.

The first tramp was to be taken that very day. Instead of going down Mount Rigi by train, as they had come up, they were going to walk. They were going to walk away down to the shore of the beautiful lake at the foot of the mountain. It was the large lake of Lucerne, but it looked like only a tiny pond, it Large umbrellas were raised over small booths on the mountain top

"Just think," said Jack, "in a few hours we shall be crossing that very lake in one of those steamers. They don't look large enough to carry people, do they?"

After an early lunch, which was eaten in an outdoor restaurant, they started to walk down the mountain. A part of the way the path was very steep. The boys raced along, for it was easier to run than to walk.

Soon they came to a place where a great mass of rocks had slipped down across the path during the last heavy rain. The boys could see where the rocks had torn up bushes and trees, as they dashed down the mountain side.

The little home of a herdsman, lower down on the mountain, had been completely buried.

When the herdsman came home after the rain was over, he found his house hidden under a load of rocks and trees. Of course, the poor man thought that his wife and six little children had all been killed, but he would not give them up until he had tried to save them.

He saw that one corner of his house was not quite covered, so he dug away the stones as fast as he could. Some friends came to help him, and at last the herdsman could hear his little children crying. This made him work even faster, for he knew that they were alive.

It did not lake long to make an opening through a broken window

It did not take the men long to make an opening through a broken window. There they found the mother and her six frightened children sitting close together in a corner of the room. The rest of the little house had been crushed in by the heavy rocks. In some way this one corner had been protected, and so the mother and her little family were saved.

Some kind herdsmen were giving the family a home until they could build another house on the mountain side.

Lower down on the trail the Overall Boys met the father and mother and oldest daughter of this family. They were making hay on one of the tiny mountain meadows or alps.

A narrow cart had been filled with the sweet, dry hay, and the father was about to haul it down the trail. He greeted the Overall Boys politely, saying in odd German, "Good evening, my boys. May you return again to our alp."

When their father told the boys what the man had said, Joe answered quickly, "Oh, thank you! May we come up to your alp some day and help you make your hay?"

And so it was arranged that the boys should climb up to the alpine meadow some day very soon, to help the herdsman make his hay.

They were going to spend two whole weeks by Lake Lucerne at the foot of the mountain, so they would have time to do many interesting things.

After leaving the herdsman and his family, the boys hurried on down the trail. It took them nearly three hours to reach the shore of the lake, where a steamer was waiting to carry them across the water to the city of Lucerne.

It was one of the steamers which the Overall Boys had seen from the top of Mount Rigi that very morning. Away up there it had looked no larger than a plaything, but they now found that it was quite a grown-up boat.

SHOPPING IN LUCERNE

So the Overall Boys had their first sail on lovely Lake Lucerne, the most famous lake in all the world.

The sun went down in a glory of color behind the city of Lucerne at the end of the long lake, and the great, round moon came hurrying up, eager to lend her light to this beautiful part of the world while the sun was away.

It was a wonderful evening. It was almost as wonderful as the evening before, when the boys had been up above the clouds on Mount Rigi.

To-night they were very tired after the long tramp down the mountain. They were too tired to look around much as they were driven quickly along the brightly lighted streets and up the hill to their boarding place.

But in the morning they were ready for anything. The first thing to interest them was breakfast. Jack led the way down the stairs to the large dining room, but it was empty. There was nothing to eat on any of the long tables.

"Oh, dear! We are too late," cried Joe. "I shall starve before noon. I know I shall."

"No, you won't," said Jack. "Look out there under the trees. The people are having a breakfast party."

"Oh, my!" cried Joe. "Are we going to eat out there, too? I hope so!"

"Father and mother are waiting for us over by the tall rose bushes," said Jack. "We can have a little table all to ourselves."

"Is it really a party, or is it just breakfast?" asked Joe.

"I expect it is just breakfast," said Jack. "Mother has said that people here in Switzerland eat out of doors whenever they can."

"Oh, goody! let's have our breakfast out here every morning," said Joe.

And so they did. Every morning when it did not rain, the Overall Boys had their breakfast of rolls and honey and hot chocolate on a small, round table in the rose garden.

They often sat in front of their shops while working

It was lots of fun. It was almost as good as a real picnic. Each morning while they were eating, they planned what they should do during the rest of the day.

Some days they spent the forenoon visiting interesting little shops. They liked to watch the pretty Swiss girls at work on their fine embroidery. These girls, dressed in their quaint Swiss costumes, often sat on the sidewalk in front of their shops while working.

But the boys liked best the carved wood shops. Sometimes they saw boys, not much older than themselves, carving jumping-jacks and bears and queer little dwarf men out of blocks of pear wood.

Many Swiss boys learn wood carving when they are quite young, so they can earn their living in that way when they are grown up.

The Overall Boys coaxed their father to buy a fine carved bear to take home with them. The bear was as tall as Joe. He sat on his hind legs, crossing his fore paws in front of him, and he looked as if he might growl any minute.

The boys' mother said the bear should stand by the front door at home, where he could hold umbrellas for people when they came to call.

"What fun we shall have when we introduce the Sunbonnet Babies to Mr. Bear!" said Joe.

"I know a fine way to do it," said Jack. "We will stand him under the big maple tree in the back yard at home. Then, the first time Molly and May come to see us, we will take them out to meet our new playmate."

"Oh, that will be great!" shouted Joe. "I can almost hear Molly and May scream now."

"Let's visit the cuckoo shop," said Jack one afternoon. "And let's try to be there when the cuckoos all come out."

"Well, then, let's go now," said Joe. "It is ten minutes of five. We shall have just time to get there before the clocks begin to strike and the cuckoos begin to call for five o'clock."

So Jack and Joe hurried down the street into the old, old part of the city. They found the little shop just in time. An old man standing in the doorway invited the boys to go in, and of course they accepted.

On the walls around the small room hung many beautiful brown clocks of all sizes. They were very different from American clocks. These clocks looked like tiny Swiss houses or chalets. There was a round clock face in the front of each chalet, and two long swinging arms hanging down below. But the clocks were all saying, tick, tick, tick, tick, just as American clocks do.

"Now watch!" cried Joe. "The doors are beginning to open. Here come the cuckoos."

And sure enough, as the boys stood looking at the clocks, a little door near the top of each swung quickly open and a tiny cuckoo bird stepped out and flapped its wings.

The clocks all began striking and the cuckoos began calling just like this:—One, cuckoo; two, cuckoo; three, cuckoo; four, cuckoo; five, cuckoo.

It was five o'clock. The cuckoo birds folded their wings and stepped quietly back into their tiny houses. The doors closed quickly in front of them and all was still once more, except for the tick, tick of the many clocks.

"We just must buy one of those cuckoo clocks to take back to America with us," said Joe.

"We must buy two of them," said Jack. "We must take one to Molly and May. They will think it is splendid."

"Let's ask father about it," said Joe. "I know he will tell us to buy one for the Sunbonnet Babies and one for Tim and Ted."

"I am going home to supper now," said Jack. "This is Saturday, and there are fireworks on the shore of the lake every Saturday evening, you know."

"Oh, so there are!" cried Joe. "I had almost forgotten about them. Let's hurry."

SATURDAY EVENING ON LAKE LUCERNE

Long before it was dark the Overall Boys were walking up and down the beautiful shore front, waiting for the first sky rocket. Hundreds of other people were waiting and watching, too. A band was playing and everybody was happy.

"Listen! The band is playing America!" cried Joe. "Three cheers for the red, white, and blue!"

"Wait a minute, Joe," said Jack. "Father says that is one of the national hymns of Switzerland. The music is the same as for our national hymn, America, but the words are different."

"It is fine, anyway, and I feel like shouting.—Three cheers for Switzerland!" said Joe.

"So do I!" said Jack. "Switzerland is a Republic and has a President, just as we have in the United States, you know. Its national motto is 'All for each, and each for all.'"

"I thought it seemed more like home than any other country over here," said Joe. "I shouldn't like to live in a country which has a King instead of a President. I like Presidents."

"But just think of it, Joe, the whole of Switzerland is only one third as large as our state of New York, and the city of New York has a million more people in it than this whole country has; father said so."

"Well, even though the country is so small," said Joe, "it has twenty-two Cantons or states, and each Canton has a special flag. I am going to buy them all for my flag collection."

"Puff! puff! There goes a sky rocket!" shouted Jack. "And there goes another! The fun has begun, Joe!"

During the next hour the boys forgot all about national hymns and Presidents and flags. They were watching fire balloons sail far out over the dark lake and disappear behind tall mountains. They were watching rockets shoot high into the sky and burst into wonderful shapes—into ships and bears and pots of flowers. They were watching the mountains glow under lovely red and blue and yellow lights. And they were imagining that they were in a fairy city, beside a fairy lake, with the wonderful mountains of Fairyland all around them.

After awhile the boys and their father got into a small boat and rowed far out on the dark fairy lake. Other boats were floating quietly about, too, each carrying a lighted Chinese lantern.

Somewhere across the water people were singing lovely Swiss songs, and all were watching the strange, fiery things in the sky above.

Mount Pilatus, which rose very high, close beside the lake, looked cold and ghostlike under the weird, blue lights.

"Would you like to hear a ghost story about Mount Pilatus, boys?" asked their father.

"Oh, of course we should! Please tell us a ghost story!" said the boys.
more fireworks
A fire balloon

"Well," began their father, "you know how Pilate, the Roman governor of Galilee, allowed Jesus to be killed. It is said that Pilate was afterward driven out of Galilee, and that he came to this part of the world and drowned himself in a lake near the top of that mountain. So the mountain was named Pilatus.

"For many hundreds of years the people about here believed that Pilate's ghost came out of the lake once a year and wandered over the mountain. To protect the people from the ghost, the government of Lucerne forbade any one to go near the lake.

"Once six bold men disobeyed this law, and they were put into prison. The people still believed that Pilate's ghost lived on the mountain, and they did not want to offend it.

"It was not until fifteen hundred years after Pilate was driven from Galilee that the government of Lucerne gave permission for four men to climb the mountain and to explore the lake. As the men did not find the ghost, they decided that at last it was quiet.

"So people have been climbing the mountain ever since, and now they even have a railroad which goes away up to the little lake. How do you suppose the old ghost likes that?"

"And what do you suppose he thinks of the fire balloons that are sailing around his head to-night?" said Joe.

Suddenly somebody screamed, and then somebody else screamed. The little boats began to hurry and scurry in every direction. It looked as if all the Chinese lanterns had gone crazy.

Everybody's eyes were turned toward the sky, for up there, right above them, was a fire balloon. The fire had caught in the top of the balloon, and it was all ablaze.

Now this blazing balloon was falling straight down, down, down, toward the little boats on the lake. Of course the boats were scurrying to get out of the way, and of course the people screamed.

Each thought that the burning balloon would surely fall right into his boat, but it did not. It fell hissing and sputtering into the dark waters, right where the boats had been only a few moments before.

"Well, that was a narrow escape!" exclaimed Jack. "We can imagine now how it would seem to be in a falling flying machine. I think I don't care to try it."

Then, with many other boats, they rowed quickly back to the brightly lighted city, and the boys were soon sound asleep, resting for the next day's fun.

THE BIRTHDAY PARTY

Now the next day was Joe's birthday, and he was to have a real Swiss party. At least, he was going with a dozen Swiss boys and their schoolmaster for a long tramp up the mountain side behind Lucerne. Jack was going, too.

The boys were hardly through breakfast on the birthday morning, when they heard the beating of a drum in the street. In a moment the high garden gate swung open, and in marched a procession of jolly boys.

The leader of the procession was the drummer boy. A great St. Bernard dog bounded along beside him.

These boys could all speak a little English, and as Jack and Joe had learned some German, they had no trouble in talking with each other, though sometimes it was hard for the St. Bernard dog to understand their language.

The drummer boy and the schoolmaster and the dog led the way, while the other boys followed, two by two

The Overall Boys put on their knapsacks and quickly joined the procession. The drummer boy and the schoolmaster and the dog led the way, while the other boys followed, two by two.

Swiss boys nearly always carry knapsacks or botany cans on their backs when they are tramping. They like to gather and study the wild flowers and plants that grow by the way. Of course they always carry fresh rolls and sweet chocolate in their knapsacks, too.

These boys think nothing is so good for lunch as rolls and sweet chocolate, and the Overall Boys are sure that they are right. They are also sure that no other sweet chocolate is as good as that made in Switzerland.

The Swiss schoolboys often wear soft green felt hats with bunches of mountain flowers or long feathers standing straight up behind. So the Overall Boys bought feathers for their hats, too.

In passing through the town the schoolmaster took the boys to see their famous national monument, the Lion of Lucerne.

High on a natural wall of rock they saw the figure of a great dying lion, with a broken spear in his side. At the foot of the wall there is a small, dark pond with green trees around it, making a quiet and beautiful spot.

The schoolmaster told the boys how, many years before, some brave Swiss guards had given their lives to protect the palace of the French King, Louis XVI, in his beautiful city of Paris.

High on a natural wall of rock they saw the famous national monument, the Lion of Lucerne

He told them how this national monument had later been made by a great artist in memory of the soldiers who were as brave as lions, and who were not afraid to die at their post.

After leaving the lion, the boys marched down the steep, crooked streets toward the river. Mount Pilatus rose high in front of them, a soft, white cloud above his head.

"We are sure of fine weather to-day, boys," said the master. "Pilatus is wearing his hood.
'If Pilatus wears his hood,
Then the weather's always good.'"

"He is celebrating my birthday," said Joe. "Of course the weather must be good to-day."

As the boys tramped on they passed a number of small milk carts bringing barrels of fresh, rich milk into the city. The milk had been sent down from the high mountain pastures, where the cattle spend the summer months.

Each milk cart was drawn by two strong dogs and a man. The dogs seemed very proud of their work. They knew every house where they must stop to leave the morning's milk.

In a few minutes the party was crossing a queer, crooked bridge over the river. It is called the Chapel Bridge. On its roof and walls there are more than one hundred and fifty pictures, which were painted a long, long time ago.

Right beside the bridge, standing in the river, is a very old stone tower. The schoolmaster said that this tower was probably once used as a lighthouse.

The Overall Boys were very much interested in the quaint old covered bridge, but they were even more interested in some beautiful white swans swimming in the water below it.

"The swans are hunting for their breakfast," said Joe. "I am going to give them one of my nice rolls."

Then Joe ran quickly through the bridge and down to the edge of the river. He took one of the fresh, long rolls from his knapsack and broke it into small bits, which he threw into the water.
feeding swans
He took one of the fresh, long rolls from his knapsack and fed the swans on the river

In a moment the lovely white swans were sailing swiftly toward him. They bowed their long, graceful necks in many a pretty "Thank you" for the generous breakfast.

At last the procession tramped out through a low gate under a large watch tower on the old city wall. Soon they were climbing up through the beautiful woods on the mountain side.

They found many interesting plants and flowers to study, and they were glad of the sweet chocolate and rolls in their knapsacks.

But the real fun came when they reached the restaurant high on the mountain. One of the boys kept Joe out of sight while the others helped arrange a table for the birthday dinner.

It was a large, round table, and it stood out of doors on a high terrace, where they could look far down upon the little city of Lucerne, and upon the beautiful lake surrounded by the great mountains.

The boys took from their knapsacks a number of small packages, which they had kept a secret from Joe.

"Let's arrange all of our presents around Joe's plate," said Jack. "And let's put a bunch of alpine roses in the center of the table."

In a few moments a procession of carved wooden bears and queer little dwarf men were marching around Joe's plate, while on the plate were piled the other presents.

There was a handsome jackknife; a pocket book containing a silver franc piece, which is the same as twenty cents; a tiny Swiss chalet with a real music box inside of it; and best of all, a beautiful little Swiss watch,—one which would keep perfect time,—besides cakes and cakes of delicious sweet chocolate.

When everything was ready, the boys stood behind their chairs around the table and sang a birthday song, while Joe was led back to the terrace by his little Swiss friend.

Poor Joe! He was so surprised and so happy he did not know what to do or what to say, but he really said the very nicest thing: "Thank you, thank you, everybody! Oh, ich danke euch allen!" Then he sat down quickly in his chair and began looking at his many presents.

But he could not look at his presents long, for he had to think about the delicious birthday dinner that was being served. There was everything that hungry boys could wish for, from real chicken to ice cream and cake. And there was a box of chocolate candy for each boy to take home with him.

A Swiss band played lovely music all the while they were eating, and the schoolmaster told them wonderful stories about his life on the high Alps when he was a little boy.

The boys ate so long, and they ate so much, the schoolmaster finally told them that they must stop soon or they would not be able to tramp back down the mountain.

There was no need to be anxious, however, for they all tramped down better than they had tramped up.

Joe did not complain once because of the extra weight in his knapsack. It had been the finest birthday that he had ever known.

WILLIAM TELL AND HIS LITTLE SON

Early next morning the Overall Boys and their parents went aboard a small steamer which would carry them to the other end of the long, narrow lake of Lucerne.

They hurried quickly to the front upper deck, for they had long ago learned that this was the best place for sightseeing; and they knew that during the next few hours they would see some of the loveliest scenery in the whole world.

"I believe this will be the finest trip we have had yet," said Joe.

"I know it will be the finest one!" exclaimed Jack. "I should rather see the spot where William Tell shot the apple from his little boy's head, than any other spot in Switzerland."

"Oh, I shouldn't!" said Joe. "I should rather climb one of those great mountains all covered with snow, and take a walk on a real glacier."

"Well, some day perhaps we can do that, too," said Jack. "But I don't want to do it to-day. I want to hear the story which father is going to tell us, about how William Tell and his little boy helped to make Switzerland a free country."

"Oh, yes, father! Do tell us the story while we are sailing up the very lake where a part of it happened," said Joe.

"All right," said their father. "This is the story:

"More than six hundred years ago the people of Switzerland did not govern themselves, as they do now. A part of the people were governed by the King of Austria. Austria is a large country northeast of Switzerland, you know.

"Now the King of Austria could not live here and govern the people himself, so he sent one of his men to be their Governor. The name of the last Governor was Gessler.

The Overall Boys hear the story of William Tell

"This man Gessler was a very proud and cruel Governor. He made the people do many things which they did not think were right.

"One of the strange things which Gessler did was to have a hat placed on a tall pole in the marketplace of the little village of Altdorf. He then commanded every one who passed through the marketplace to bow before the hat, just as if the King of Austria were sitting there.

"A watchman stood near by to take the names of any who did not obey the command.

"Of course the people were much excited, but they did not dare to disobey the Governor. At least no one dared to do so until, one day, William Tell came to the marketplace. He was a proud and brave man. He thought it was foolish to bow to a hat on a pole, so he walked straight by it without bowing.

"When Gessler heard what William Tell had done, he was very angry. As a punishment, he commanded Tell to shoot an apple placed on the head of his favorite son, Walter. If the arrow went through the apple, Tell's life was to be spared. But if he missed the mark, he and his little boy were to die.

"Gessler knew that William Tell could shoot an arrow straighter than any other man in the country, but he thought that his courage would fail, with his own little boy standing just under the mark. And it almost did fail. But Walter called, 'Shoot, father! I am not afraid! I will stand very still!'

"So Tell placed an arrow in his crossbow and another one in his belt. Gessler stood the boy under a tree some distance away, and placed an apple on his head. He then commanded Tell to shoot.

"In a moment Tell's arrow had gone straight through the center of the apple.

"The people, who were watching, shouted for joy, because the lives of William Tell and his brave little son were saved. Even Gessler was forced to praise Tell for his wonderful skill.

"'But,' said Gessler, 'you must tell me why you put the second arrow in your belt.'

"Tell did not wish to answer this question, but Gessler promised he should not lose his life.

"'Well, sir,' answered Tell, 'as you have promised to spare my life, I will tell you the truth. If I had missed the apple and shot my boy, the second arrow should have gone through your heart.'

"'Ah!' said Gessler. 'I have promised to spare your life, but you shall be put where you will never again see the sun nor the moon. Then I shall be safe from your swift arrows.'

"So William Tell was quickly bound with ropes and taken to the boat on which Gessler was to cross the lake in returning to his castle.

"While they were on the water a terrible storm came up. It seemed as if they would all be drowned. The boatmen begged Gessler to take the ropes from their prisoner, so that he might help them bring the boat ashore.

Boys looking at picture of Tell story
As he sprang, he gave the boat a strong push with his foot, back into the rough water again

"So Gessler commanded that Tell be untied and that he guide them to safety.

"Tell had been on this lake in storms many times before, and he knew where the few safe landing places were. He knew there was a large flat rock, close under the steep shore, on to which one could easily spring from a boat, so he skillfully steered in its direction.

"When a great wave swung the tossing boat quite close to the flat rock, Tell seized his crossbow and sprang out. As he sprang, he gave the boat a strong push with his foot, back into the rough water again.

"Brave Tell was free. He climbed quickly through the woods and up the steep mountain side. At last he came to the path Gessler would have to take in returning to his castle, if he were not drowned on the stormy lake.

"Here Tell waited and thought. He was waiting to see if Gessler would come, and he was thinking about the brave people who were being so cruelly treated by their Austrian Governor. He was willing, if necessary, to give his life to bring freedom to his country.

"At last Gessler and his men came hurrying up the path toward the castle. They had escaped the storm.

"As Tell stood hidden behind some bushes near the path he saw Gessler refuse to help a poor woman and her little children. The woman had come to beg the Governor to release her husband, who had been unjustly put into prison. Gessler would not listen to her, and the unhappy woman went away weeping.

"Tell was now sure that it was his duty to save his people from their suffering. So he let fly a swift arrow from his bow and it hit the mark, as his arrows always did.

"That was the last of Austrian Governors for Switzerland. The people have been free and have governed themselves ever since, and that, you know, is more than six hundred years," said the boys' father.

"Isn't it wonderful to be as brave as William Tell was!" said Jack after a moment.

"And isn't it wonderful to be as brave as Walter was!" said Joe. "I wonder if I could be as brave as that!"
apple with arrow through it

A VISIT TO TELL'S COUNTRY

While the boys were listening to this interesting story, the steamer was carrying them slowly up the beautiful lake toward the very places where it all happened.

At last they came to a narrow part of the lake where the mountains rose steep and high on both sides.

"Look, boys!" said their father. "Do you see the little chapel just ahead of us, on the left? It is called Tell's Chapel, because it is built on the flat rock on to which Tell sprang from Gessler's boat that stormy day. On the walls inside of the chapel an artist has painted four large pictures showing the whole story of William Tell."

"Oh, father, please let us go ashore here," said Jack. "I want to look at those pictures."

"Do you see the little chapel just ahead of us?"

"And I want to climb up into the dark woods behind the chapel," said Joe.

"All right," said their father. "How would you like to walk the rest of the way to the end of the lake? It is only two or three miles. I am sure you never have walked over so beautiful a road as this one."

"Oh, do let us walk!" shouted Joe. "It will be lots more fun than sitting still here on the steamer."

So they went ashore right near the little chapel. First, they looked at the pictures that told the story of Tell and Gessler, on the walls inside of the chapel. Then they followed a steep, narrow path that led up the mountain side through the dark woods. This path soon brought them to a pretty garden restaurant.

Of course they were all very thirsty, so they sat around a small table under the great trees and drank raspberry lemonade, which was served to them in very tall glasses. Raspberry lemonade, as it is made in Switzerland, is much nicer than plain lemonade, at least so the Overall Boys thought.

A few minutes later they began their tramp over one of the most beautiful roads in the world. It is called the Axenstrasse, because it is built along the side of the steep mountain called the Axenberg.

A part of the way the mountain is so steep the road could not be built on the outside of it, so a tunnel has been cut right through the rocky side. Here and there the outer wall of rock has been cut away, making great arches through which people can look out over the beautiful lake to the high mountains beyond.

The great arches from which people can see the high mountains beyond

The famous St. Gotthard railroad is also built along this mountain side. In some places the trains glide along the steep mountain almost straight above the deep lake, and in other places they pass through long, dark tunnels.

The carriage road over which the Overall Boys were tramping was as smooth and level as a floor. Many automobiles flew past the happy walking party, but the boys did not envy the people who were riding in them. They could see and enjoy everything, while those who had to ride missed a great deal.

They passed through two or three small villages, where the narrow balconies on the pretty chalets were all covered with beautiful climbing roses.

In the center of a fountain, in one of the small flower gardens, the boys saw the figure of a queer little dwarf with a large, red umbrella over his head.

"Oh, Jack, see that little man standing in the fountain!" cried Joe. "He looks like the good dwarfs we read about in fairy tales. See what a small body he has, and what a large head!"

"And do look at his long beard and his high, pointed cap!" said Jack. "How proud he is of his big, red umbrella! He stands in the center of the fountain with the water falling all around, but not a drop falls on him."

"Isn't he a jolly old fellow! I suppose he brings good luck to the people who own that garden," said Joe. "In fairy tales the mountain dwarfs always bring good luck, if they are treated kindly."

"Well, this old fellow looks as if he were enjoying his lovely garden home," said Jack.

At last the trampers came to a small town where there was a high coach drawn by four horses waiting to carry people two miles up the valley, to the village of Altdorf.

Travelers usually go to Altdorf by train now, but the Overall Boys chose to ride on top of the high coach. The Overall Boys chose to ride on top of the high coach

It was a beautiful drive, and everybody was happy and hungry when the coach drew up to a small hotel in the famous little village.

Supper was served in the hotel garden, then the boys went to bed to dream of William Tell and his brave son, Walter, who had once walked the streets of this very village.

Quite early next morning, two eager little boys were standing in the old marketplace They were looking at the tall bronze monument of William Tell and his little son.

"Think of it!" said Joe. "William Tell stood on this very spot when he shot the apple from Walter's head."

"Yes," said Jack. "And Walter stood away back there, where the fountain now is."

"My! I know I should have trembled, if I had been in Walter's place," said Joe.

"I am sure Walter did not tremble. See how brave and happy he looks, as he stands up there with his father's hand on his shoulder. He was proud to help save his father's life. He was even willing to die to save him. Why, I should be willing to do as much for my father, if he were in trouble," said Jack.

"So should I!" cried Joe. "No one shall ever hurt father or mother, if I can help it!"

"Well, that sounds good," said their father, who came up behind the boys just in time to hear what they were talking about. "I shall not be afraid to serve my country, so long as I have boys as brave as Walter Tell."

They were looking at the monument of William Tell

"Oh, father, did this all really happen, or is it just a story?" asked Jack.

"Well," said their father, "a few wise men are telling us that it is only a legend, but many of the Swiss people believe that it is every bit true. They are proud to have had such heroes as William Tell and his little boy."

"Of course they are," said Joe. "I am going to believe that it is true. Why, William Tell did almost as much for his country as George Washington did for ours. I think that he ought to be called the 'Father of his Country,' the same as Washington is."

"So do I," said their father. "But let me tell you something now. I have a surprise for you. The people of the village are going to play the story of William Tell to-day in their little open-air theater on the edge of the woods.

"The king's hat will be there on a pole in the center of the busy marketplace, and all the people will bow low to it—all except William Tell and his little son, who will march proudly by it. Then, of course, Tell will have to shoot the apple from his little boy's head, and he will be taken across the stormy lake in Gessler's boat, and then he will spring out upon the rocky shore, and escape into the woods. Gessler and his men will climb up the mountain path toward the castle; the poor woman will beg Gessler to release her husband from prison—and all the rest of the story will be played. Would you like to see it?"

"Oh, of course we should!" exclaimed the boys. "We should rather see it than anything else we can think of."

And when they had seen it, they wanted to see it all right over again.

OVER AND THROUGH THE MOUNTAINS

Slowly, slowly up the mountain crept the long train. It was carrying the Overall Boys far away from lovely Lake Lucerne. It was taking them over the wonderful Brünig Pass. It was carrying them even more slowly down, down the steep slope on the other side toward the head of the deep valley, where lay the pretty Swiss village of Meiringen.

They glided over high bridges

As the boys stood by the car window they could see the long line of track far below them. Sometimes when their train passed a sharp curve, they could even see the engine at one end of the train and the last car at the other end.

They glided over high bridges above torrents of water which dashed down the mountain to join the blue lake in the valley below.

It was wonderful—the mountains, the torrents, the lakes, and the strong train which carried them over everything! It was all so wonderful, the boys had no words to express their delight. For the first time on their long journey they were almost silent.

Once in a while one of the boys would cry: "Look at that great waterfall!" or "See the precipice right below us!" or "Watch us cross that high bridge!"

It was much more exciting than the ride in the thunder storm up Mount Rigi, but at last even this ride came to an end.

Yes, the wonderful ride over the Brünig Pass ended at Meiringen, but the more wonderful tramp over the Great Scheidegg Pass was to begin at Meiringen, and the boys were to have other strange experiences down in the deep, green valley. The most exciting of them all came the very next morning.

There was an early breakfast eaten in the pretty garden of the hotel, then their father said:

"Now for the fun! Yesterday we went over a mountain. To-day we shall go through one."

The boys had no words to express their delight

"Are we going through a tunnel?" cried Joe.

"No, indeed!" said their father. "At least it is not a tunnel made by men. Come and see what you think of it."

They were soon tramping along the village street toward the high mountain at the head of the narrow valley. A swift river hurried past them to join the lake at the other end of the valley. It was the river Aar.

The boys saw where the river had overflowed its banks in the springtime, when the snows melted and the heavy rains came. They were told that the bridges were often washed away, and that sometimes great masses of rocks came tearing down the mountain side, right into the little village, crushing and burying everything in their path.

The party quickly left the village far behind them, and each step brought them nearer to the high mountain wall close ahead.

"How shall we get over that mountain, father?" asked Joe. "Shall we have to climb to the top?"

"No, Joe," said his father. "We shall do no climbing to-day. I believe we can go through it, if this swift river can."

"Of course we can!" shouted Jack. "Let's follow the river."

So they followed a footpath along the banks of the noisy river. Soon the banks began to grow high and steep. At last they rose straight up on both sides, until the boys could see only a narrow strip of blue sky far above them.

"The mountain has cracked open!" shouted Joe. "We are in the crack!"

"So we are!" cried Jack. "I believe the river did it. See it come tearing along!"

The path through the mountain

"Look ahead of us!" said Joe. "There isn't room even for a path. A board walk has been fastened with iron rods to the wall. It hangs right over the rushing water. What if it should break while we are on it! I am not sure that I want to go any farther."

"Come, now, don't be a coward, Joe," said his father. "The Swiss government builds these paths, and they are built strong. We are safe."

So on they tramped through the great crack in the mountain. In some places the path hung high over the swift waters. In other places it was tunneled through the dark rocks. But always it followed the deep, narrow crack, with the noisy river at its bottom and a bit of blue sky far, far above.

For nearly a mile the boys followed this path. In many places the river was so noisy they had to shout to make each other hear. But at last they came out on the other side of the mountain.

They had not climbed the mountain, and they had not gone around it. They had gone through it. And more wonderful still, the great river Aar has been carrying its waters through the mountain for ages and ages.

Close beside the river, at the end of the path, was a tiny shop kept by a little old woman and her granddaughter.

The little girl served the boys to raspberry lemonade, and she sold them picture post cards showing the strange path over which they had just come.

Then back they went into the mountain crack—over the footpath hanging high above the rushing water, and through the small, dark tunnels, until once more they were in the lovely green valley of Meiringen. village

REAL TRAMPERS

Next morning the boys were up with the sun, for there was a long journey ahead of them. It was not to be a journey by train nor by boat. It was to be a journey on foot.

The party was to follow a trail over the high mountain range which shuts in the deep valley of the river Aar on the south. The trail would lead them over the Great Scheidegg Pass and down into the beautiful valleys on the other side.

They were going to spend at least a week on the way. There would be so many interesting things to see and to do, they would not want to hurry.

The boys carried knapsacks on their backs, in which they put the few things they would need while crossing the mountains. They were real trampers at last.
hiknig on path with fences on either side
They carried knapsacks on their backs, in which they put the few things they would need while crossing the mountains

The first part of the trail was very steep. The little party climbed up and up, until the village, far below them, looked very small indeed.

After awhile they heard a strange rumbling noise, which grew louder and louder the higher they climbed. Soon it became a roar, and right above their path they saw a tremendous waterfall tumbling down over the steep mountain side. It fairly made the rocks tremble, it fell with such force, and the air was filled with a fine, wet spray.

The boys sprang up the path close beside the great waterfall. When they reached the top of it they were a very wet but a very jolly party.

"Well, that's the most fun we have had yet!" shouted Joe. "I should like to do it right over again."

"I shouldn't," said a little girl who was standing near by. "I have to come up here every few days. I don't like to get so wet."

"Why do you come up so often?" asked Jack.

"I go down to the village to buy bread for mother. I live up here. That is our chalet up there by the brook. My name is Gretel."

"Do you go down to the village to school, too?" asked Joe.

"Yes," answered the little girl. "But this is vacation time now. I often take another path when I go to school. Sometimes I ride home on that big car, which helps me up the mountain as far as the waterfall."

"Do you go to school all winter?" asked Jack.

"Oh, yes! except when the snow is so deep I just can't get there. All of us girls and boys have to go to school forty weeks every year. I am glad we do. I like to go to school."

"Please let us carry that basket of bread for you," said Jack. "I think our path goes right by your house."

So the children walked on up the path together, and Gretel told the boys many interesting things about her life on the mountain alp.

"I always thought a Swiss alp was a high mountain peak," said Joe.

"Oh, no! An alp is a lovely mountain meadow," said Gretel. "See what a fine great alp ours is. This is one of the low alps. Father raises lots of hay here to feed the cows during the long winter."

"Where are your cows now?" asked Jack.

Gretel's home was a pretty, brown chalet, whose roof was covered with large stones to keep it from being blown away

"They are feeding farther up on the higher alps," said Gretel. "Father takes them up early every summer, and they don't come down until fall."

"Do you think we shall see them on our way over the mountains?" asked Joe.

"Yes, I am sure you will," said Gretel. "Your path goes right across the alp where father's little cabin is. My two brothers, Franz and Sep, are up there with father now. They take care of the goats, and help to milk the cows and make the cheese. I wish I were up there, too!"

"Why can't you go up with us?" asked Jack. "You could surprise your father and brothers."

"Oh, I should love to go!" cried Gretel. "I could stay with them in their little cabin for a few days, then Franz would bring me home, I know he would. I will ask mother if I may go. See, this is our chalet."

It was a pretty, brown chalet. The broad, low roof was covered with many large stones to keep it from being blown away during the great winter storms.

But now it was the lovely summer time, and Gretel's mother had set two small tables just outside her front door. She always had something good to serve to hungry trampers To-day there was a big bowl of delicious wild strawberries on each of the tables.

Of course the Overall Boys were suddenly very hungry. And how they enjoyed the bread and butter and wild strawberries and cream which Gretel's mother served to them!

After the tea party was over, Gretel showed them yards and yards of lace she was making

After the tea party was over, Gretel showed them the lace which she was making. There were yards and yards of it. The boys thought it was wonderful to see Gretel move the bobbins of thread so quickly over the big pillow, and never make mistakes in the pattern.

"I have been making lace ever since I was five years old," said Gretel. "I sell enough lace every summer to pay for all of my clothes."

"Oh, Gretel, will you sell some to us?" asked Joe. "We don't wear lace ourselves, but the Sunbonnet Babies do. They would love to wear some of your lace."

"And I should love to have them wear it. Of course I will sell you some," said Gretel.

Then the boys chose some of the very prettiest lace Gretel had made, and bought it for the Sunbonnet Babies.

"Now I want to show you where my bees live," said Gretel. And she led the boys up the hill behind her house where, under some great trees, was a row of tiny chalets.

"This is my bee village," she said. "Each bee family has a little chalet of its own. The bees fly all over our alp, gathering nectar from the flowers. Sometimes they fly very far away, hunting for more flowers, but they always come back again, bringing their baskets full of nectar.

"They work so hard, they fill their little houses brim full of honey every summer. I am sure we couldn't live without our bees. Some summers they earn more money than father can."

"There must be millions of bees in Switzerland to make so much honey," said Jack. "I believe every family here eats honey for breakfast. In America we eat cereal. I think honey is much nicer."
lady doing handwork

"Come, boys!" called their father. "It is time to go on. Gretel's mother says she may go with us as far as her father's cabin. We shall give Franz and Sep a fine surprise."

"Oh, goody!" cried Gretel. "I haven't seen Franz and Sep since they took the cows up the mountain in the spring."

"Tell us about it, Gretel," said Jack. "What happens when the cows go up the mountain?"

"Why, that is the jolliest day of the whole year," said Gretel, "except, perhaps, the day when they all come home in the fall.

"Father ties big bells around the necks of the prettiest cows, and mother and I trim their horns with flowers. Then the procession begins. This year Sep led the procession with his seven little goats. He was the proudest boy that ever went up the mountain.
following goats
Sep led the procession with his seven little goats

"The cows know what it means when the bells are tied to their necks. The summer on the alps is a long picnic for them. Mother and I go up a little way with the procession. Other families take their cows up the mountain the same day, and we sing and have a jolly time."

"Do you send all of your cows up to the higher alps in the spring?" asked Jack. "Where did you get the delicious cream that your mother gave us to-day?"

"We keep one cow at home to give us milk and cream during the summer," said Gretel. "I am always sorry for the poor cow that is left behind, she is so lonesome. We have to tie her very carefully, or she runs away. She keeps going until she finds her friends 'way up the mountain. Then, of course, father or one of the boys must bring her down again."

"Oh, Gretel, when your brothers see you coming they will think you have run away because you are so lonesome without them," said Joe, laughing.

"Well, they must keep me a week before they take me home, or I shall run away again," said Gretel. "I am lonesome without them."

And so they talked, as they tramped along together up the mountain trail. Once they met a man with a large milk can on his back. The man greeted the party with a friendly, "Guten Tag! Glückliche Reise!" This was his way of saying, "Good day! A happy journey!" So the boys quickly answered, "Danke schön!" which means, "Thank you kindly!"
wating for man with milk can to pass

Once they met a man with a large milk can on his back

Every day this man carried his can full of milk down the mountain to sell to the people who had no cows. He always greeted the strangers whom he passed on the way, and wished them a happy journey.

On and on, and up and up the little party tramped. At last they began to see snowbanks, in shaded places near the trail. Sometimes, just below a large snowbank, they found a sunny spot covered with a carpet of lovely summer flowers. There were violets and buttercups and daisies and forget-me-nots, and low bushes of small red alpine roses.

These little wild gardens were watered all summer by the melting snows. The gay flowers seemed to like the icy water at their roots.

The Overall Boys often stopped for a snowball battle with each other and with Gretel. Then from some mountain garden, they picked fresh flowers for their hats, and on they tramped.

Their trail led them below a large glacier, which lay between two high mountain peaks not far away. The boys could hear the great ice river twisting and turning in its bed, for the hot summer sun made it very uncomfortable.

Once there came a loud boom, like a cannon. The boom was followed by a crash, and the crash by a long, loud rumbling noise, which gradually died away.

"Oh, Gretel, what was that?" cried Joe. "I believe it was an earthquake."

One of the mountain alps they crossed

"Oh, no! That was not an earthquake," said Gretel, laughing. "That was a piece of the glacier breaking off. It must have had a long fall before it found a place where it could stop."

"I am glad it couldn't fall in this direction," said Jack. "I thought I wanted to take a walk on a glacier, but I am not so sure about it now."

"Oh, yes, you must!" said Gretel. "It is lots of fun. I have been up to that glacier twice with father. There are great cracks in it, so deep you can hardly see the bottom of them. It is perfectly safe to go with father. He often takes Americans up there."

"Well, I think I should rather take a walk on some other glacier. I am afraid this one is going to pieces," said Joe.

"No, it isn't!" said Gretel, laughing at Joe again. "The glacier melts and moves a little every summer, but a great deal of fresh snow falls on it every winter. I guess it will last as long as the mountains do."

THE HERDSMAN'S CABIN

It was late afternoon before the trampers reached the green alp where Gretel's father and brothers were pasturing their cows.

It was milking time. Franz and his father were milking the big, brown cows near the cabin. Sep was milking his goats. The pigs were eating their supper of skimmed milk, and Barry, the dog, was keeping his eye on them all.

It was Barry who first saw the trampers, and away he bounded to meet them. His bark was very fierce until Gretel called him by name, then he almost wagged his tail off, he was so glad to see her. He was even glad to see the strangers, because they had brought Gretel with them.

Franz and Sep and their father were just as happy as Barry to see their little Gretel and her strange friends from America.

It was milking time, and Franz and his father were milking the big, brown cows near the cabin

Soon they were all eating supper together, sitting around a rough table in the small cabin. It was a simple supper, but the hungry boys thought they never had eaten a nicer one. There was a long loaf of bread, and a great round cheese with holes all through it, and a dish of wild strawberries, and a pitcher of warm milk.

While they were eating, they suddenly heard the clear, sweet notes of a horn. The sound came from the high mountain above the cabin. In a moment the same notes came more softly from the mountain on the other side of the alp, and again still more softly they came.

Then the herdsman took his great horn, which was taller than himself, and blew a few long, clear notes on it in answer

"What is that?" cried Joe.

"It is my neighbor, who pastures his cows on the alp above us," said Gretel's father. "He is blowing his great horn to tell us that the sun is just setting behind that snow-covered peak. I must answer him, so he may know that all is well with us."

Then the herdsman took his great horn, which was taller than himself, and went out in front of his cabin. He blew a few long, clear notes, which meant, he said, "Praise ye the Lord." Again and again the same notes came back in echo from the mountain walls, each time more softly.

The snow-covered peaks were no longer white, but glowing red from the rays of the setting sun. Then darkness came on very quickly.

The tired travelers were glad to find a small inn on the alp where they could spend the night. Of course Gretel stayed with her father and brothers in their little cabin.

There were only two rooms in the cabin. The larger room belonged to the cows. They came in here to be milked in stormy weather. In the other room the family cooked and ate and made their cheeses. Their bedroom was a low balcony over one end of this room, and they reached it by climbing up a short ladder.

Early the next morning Jack and Joe went with Sep and his goats up the rocky mountain side

Next morning the boys were wakened early by Sep calling to them outside of their window.

"Oh, Jack and Joe," he called, "come with me. I have to take my goats up the mountain to their pasture. There is something fine up there that I want to show you."

So Jack and Joe went with Sep and his goats up the rocky mountain side. It was a hard climb, but it was fun.

The little goats could climb anywhere. They went into dangerous places where the cows could not go, and they found many tender bits of grass to eat.

When the boys had climbed very high, Sep crept carefully out on a narrow shelf of rock. He lay face downward and reached far over the edge. The mountain side was very steep below him.

"Watch me, boys!" he cried. "But don't you come too near."

Then, very carefully, he picked a small, furry, white flower which was growing on the steep, rocky wall. He picked another and another of the flowers, until his hand was full of them.

"There now!" he cried. "You know my secret. I have shown you where my edelweiss grows. It grows only in the most dangerous places on the high mountains. I pick a few of the flowers every day, when they are in bloom, to sell to travelers who cross our alp, but you are the only people I have ever brought up here to see them growing."

"Oh, thank you, Sep!" cried Jack. "We'll never, never tell your secret. But please let us pick a few of the flowers ourselves."

So each of the boys carried down the mountain a handful of the proud little flowers which they had picked themselves.

The Overall Boys were real mountain climbers at last, for only mountain climbers ever find and pick the edelweiss.

When the boys reached the cabin, Sep's father was watching a great kettle of milk, over an open fire. He had put more than a hundred quarts of milk into the copper kettle, with a little rennet to make it turn into curd.

Herdsmen make their rennet by soaking a calf's stomach in water or in whey; they then save this liquid to use in making their cheeses.

Sep's father stirred and watched the milk in his great copper kettle until the curd began to form. He then swung the kettle away from the fire, and put both bare arms into the warm milk. He worked the cheese into one large lump, and lifted it out on a great tray, where he worked it still more to squeeze out the milk.

Sep's father stirred and watched the milk in his great copper kettle until the curd began to form

It was then put into a round, wooden press a few days. Each day the press was opened and the cheese rubbed with salt.

When it was just right, it would be taken out and laid on a shelf in the small cheese house, where all the cheeses were kept until they could be carried down the mountain and sold. But they were not really good to eat until they were at least six months old.

Sep's father made one of these cheeses every day, and he made cheeses from his goats' milk, too. He and his boys lived a busy life on the mountain. They had no time to be lonesome.

The Overall Boys told Franz and Sep how they often had Swiss cheese for dinner in America. They said when they got home again they should certainly tell their grocer just how his big Swiss cheeses were made.
Rolling churn

A SUMMER BLIZZARD

The travelers spent two happy days with their friends in the herdsman's cabin. They would like to have spent the rest of the summer with them. Jack and Joe would like to have learned how to milk the goats and how to blow the great alpine horn.

But there were many other things which they wanted to do and to see in this wonderful little country of Switzerland, so they shouldered their knapsacks and started once more on the trail.

The way soon became steep and rocky. Gray clouds hid the snow-covered peaks. The wind blew cold, and the boys were glad of the hard climb to keep themselves warm.

They crossed one or two small alps where cows were feeding, and they stopped at a tiny cabin to ask for a drink of milk.

In the cabin they found a small boy, who was watching a large kettle of milk over an open fire. The boy said that his father had gone up the mountain to hunt for a lost cow, so he was making cheese from his goats' milk.

The Overall Boys were quite sure that they would be lonesome, if they had to stay away up there all alone. But this little boy whistled and sang and talked with his goats, calling them each by name. They really were having a jolly time together.

After the good drink of milk the travelers tramped on and up, while the gray clouds dropped lower and the wind grew colder. Soon fine white flakes began to frisk through the air and to dance on the boys' cheeks.

"Oh, Jack," called Joe, "it is snowing!"

"So it is!" shouted Jack. "It's snowing! It's really snowing, and it's summer time! Hurrah!"

The white flakes fell faster and thicker. In a few moments they were falling so fast and so thick the trampers could see only a short way ahead of them. It was hard climbing now. The path was steep and slippery. The boys had to stop often to get their breath, and their knapsacks suddenly grew very heavy.

"I suppose it is because we are up so high," said Jack. "The air is so thin up here we can't get enough of it to breathe. It is always like that on the high mountains, they say."

"I don't care," said Joe. "We are in a snow blizzard, anyhow. Just think of it!"

"I shouldn't care to lose our path," said Jack. "I guess it wouldn't be a very happy night for us if we did."

"Oh, Jack, I have lost the path already! I can hardly see you. My! How it snows! Where are father and mother?"

"Here we are!" shouted their father. "I think we are near the top of the Pass. I hear a dog barking. There is a house up at the top, where we can stay all night. Keep climbing, boys!"

Just then a great dog came bounding down the mountain toward them. He gave a short, quick bark, turned about and led the party safely up to the small hotel. Then away he bounded again to find other travelers, who might be lost in the snow and who needed his help. He was a St. Bernard dog, and he had saved the lives of many people on the high mountains.

It was a tired party that spent the night in the little hotel at the top of the Great Scheidegg Pass, but when morning came they were ready for another battle with the snow.

Of course the trail was covered, and the snow was too soft and too deep for them to tramp over it without snowshoes. The little party was snow-bound on the mountains in midsummer.

But the Overall Boys liked being snow-bound. They built a fine snow fort, with snow soldiers in it, and piles of snow cannon balls to keep enemies away from the little hotel.

The St. Bernard dog had a jolly time, too. Once he jumped against one of the snow soldiers, and over they went together. After that he seemed to be afraid of the soldiers and would not go near the fort, but

The Overall Boys and the dog enjoying the snow

Next morning the boys were out early to take a look at things.

"Oh, Jack," shouted Joe, "it froze in the night! There is a hard crust over everything!"

"So there is!" said Jack. "We don't need snowshoes now. We can go down the mountain on the crust."

And that is what they did. With the St. Bernard dog to show them the way, the party hurried down over the snow before the warm sun had time to soften the crust.

As they went lower, the snow rapidly grew less. Soon the boys saw lovely bluebells and alpine roses and other flowers holding their heads bravely up through the thin, white blanket.

A few moments later their own trail came in sight. It was no longer hidden by the snow. The St. Bernard dog gave a loud bark, wagged his tail, and bounded back up the mountain. His work for that party was done.

EXPLORING A GLACIER

The rest of the way down the mountain was easy tramping.

The path soon led by the end of the great Upper Wetterhorn Glacier, and the Overall Boys begged their father to let them explore it.

"All right," said their father. "Just step into this small car and we will go on an exploring trip."

Before the boys knew what was happening, the tiny square car rose from the ground and began moving slowly upward, following the steep slope of the mountain.

"Oh, Jack, where are we going?" cried Joe. "This car is built bottom side up. The wheels are on the top of it, instead of on the bottom."

"That's so!" exclaimed Jack. "We are hanging in the air on a cable. It is lifting us right up the mountain side. And look away up there! Another car just like this one is coming down. My! Do you suppose we shall go as high as that?"

"We are hanging in the air on a cable," Jack exclaimed. "It is lifting us right up the mountain side"

"I hope so," said Joe. "But see what is below us. It is the glacier! Look at the great cracks in it. Do you hear that noise, Jack? It sounds like thunder."

"I guess it is only another crack bursting open," said Jack. "This hot sun makes the glacier move faster, and so it cracks open."

Up, up, climbed the car, right over the glacier, until it came to a wild goat's path on a narrow shelf of the mountain, more than twelve hundred feet above the starting point.

Here it slipped into a small station, and everybody stepped out. Other people took their places, and then the car moved slowly downward, leaving the boys on the steep mountain side.

"My! That was great!" cried Jack. "Now what are we going to do?"

"We are going to walk across the glacier, aren't we, father?" said Joe.

"Of course we are. We have come up here to explore it, you know," said their father.

And they did explore 'way across the great ice river. In many places they had to walk very carefully, or they would have fallen into one of the deep cracks, but at last they came safely to the other side. There was no car on this side of the glacier to carry them down the mountain, but there were long ladders to help them over the very hardest and steepest places.

There was no car on this side of the glacier, but there were long ladders to help them over the steepest places

They had to climb over great ridges of rocks, which the glacier had torn away from the higher mountains years and years before. These rocks had been brought slowly down on the ice, and dropped along the sides and end of the glacier.

At last the party came to the place where the sun and the warm winds changed the glacier from a river of ice to a river of water.

"Well, boys," said their father, "we have had a look at the outside of the glacier; now let us take a look at the inside of it." So a man threw warm blankets over their shoulders, and they entered a long, narrow passage through a hole in the ice wall.

This passage led into a beautiful, blue ice room. The floor was ice, the walls were ice, and the ceiling was ice. There was no lamp in the room, and yet it was not dark.

"Isn't it beautiful!" cried Joe. "Think of it, we are in the center of a great ice river. There is nothing but ice all around us."

"I know it," said Jack. "I am sure the glaciers are the most wonderful things in Switzerland, but I have stayed inside of this one as long as I want to. I should rather be tramping."

AUF WIEDERSEHEN

And so they tramped on. They spent several days in the lovely village of Grindelwald. They explored glaciers. They saw waterfalls nearly a thousand feet high. They played games with the village boys and girls.

They even went almost to the top of the great Jungfrau mountain, over its wonderful railroad. The highest part of this railroad is built through a tunnel, for the surface of the mountain is covered always with snow and ice.

The train carried them nearly twelve thousand feet above the ocean. They were twice as high up as they were on the top of Mount Rigi. There were miles and miles of snow and ice all around them, and great banks of snow-white clouds in the blue sky close above.

They could see many high peaks covered with snow fields and glaciers, and lower mountains covered with green forests and alpine pastures. They had glimpses into deep, narrow valleys with muddy rivers rushing through them. Here and there were big, broad valleys dotted with villages and farms, and beautiful blue lakes, while the busy railroad trains looked like worms creeping over the hills and down the valleys. It was a wonderful view.

The Overall Boys learned more about the geography of Switzerland in a few minutes from this high mountain than they had learned during all the days of travel lower down. They never will forget what they saw while there.

But the vacation days were over at last. The boys had visited only a small part of the wonderful little country, but they had seen enough of it to make them want to spend another summer vacation in just the same way. They are sure that Switzerland is the very finest playground in the whole world, and a great many other people think so, too.

As the train hurried them far away from the high, snow-covered mountains, the boys stood by the car windows, watching and enjoying everything.

They passed ripe grain fields, in which wild scarlet poppies and tall bluebells were growing.

Close by these wild-flower gardens there was often a row of tiny chalets, where swarms of bees lived and made their delicious honey.

The train passed also through many villages of larger chalets, with broad red roofs and vine-covered balconies. In front of these pretty homes sat women and little girls working at their lace and fine embroidery.

Now and then they saw groups of small boys carrying goatskin book sacks on their backs, for the short summer vacation was over, and the Swiss schools had begun.

In a flower garden, near one of the stations, a mountain dwarf waved a Swiss flag in farewell to the passing travelers. But the nicest good-by came from a row of boys and girls sitting on a fence near the railroad track. They were selling wild flowers to travelers, as the trains stopped at their station. They shouted the names in German, French, and English—"Alpine roses, primroses, edelweiss, daisies, buttercups!"—and they eagerly begged the travelers to buy.

Of course Jack and Joe bought their hands full, for these might be the last Swiss flowers they would have for a very long time.

As the train moved on, the boys and girls, sitting on the fence, waved their hands and shouted, "Auf Wiedersehen! Glückliche Reise!"

And the Overall Boys shouted back, "Good-by! Good-by, until we meet again!"

A LETTER

Dear Boys and Girls:

I expect you will agree with the Overall Boys that nowhere else can there be quite so many wonderful things to see and to do, as there are in Switzerland.

Massachusetts and New Hampshire are very small states, you know, but together they are larger than the whole of Switzerland, and more people live in these two small states than live in Switzerland to-day.

One fourth of this famous little country is covered with lakes and rivers and glaciers, and nearly another fourth with great forests, while a large part of the remaining land is used as pasturage for a million and a half cows.

Raising cows and making cheese is the principal industry, but the clever Swiss people have many other prosperous industries as well. They make fine silks and ribbons and marvelous little watches and music boxes and jewelry and delicious sweet chocolate. Some of the men do fine wood carving, and the women do beautiful embroidery.

One of the most important lines of work is hotel keeping. Many thousands of strangers visit Switzerland every year. In winter they go there for the skating and sleighing and snowshoeing and skiing and to enjoy the bracing mountain air. In summer they do what the Overall Boys did, besides many other interesting things.

Travelers spend so much money in Switzerland, and the people who live there work so hard, they have become the richest people in the world.

Swiss schools are especially fine. Children are obliged to attend school from the time they are six years old until they are fifteen or sixteen years old.

In summer the schools begin at seven o'clock in the morning and in winter at eight o'clock, holding four hours. During the winter months there is also a session of three hours each afternoon in the week, excepting two. On these two afternoons the boys are given other work to do, and the girls attend sewing classes. They have no regular holiday, but must go to school six days every week. The boys do a great deal of gymnasium work in the winter, which keeps them strong and trains them to be mountain guides and hunters and herdsmen.

There are three national languages in Switzerland—German and French and Italian. German is used much more than French or Italian, but nearly all Swiss boys and girls learn to speak at least two languages. Sometimes they learn three or four. In fact it is said that Swiss people learn to speak languages more perfectly than any other people in the world. They are certainly among the best educated and most courageous people in the world.

The Overall Boys learned a great deal while traveling in that beautiful little country, and they are glad to share it all with you.
Sincerely your friend,
Eulalie Osgood Grover